Oliver Twist

Charles Dickens

Retold by
Mary Sebag-Montefiore

Illustrated by Barry Ablett

Reading Consultant: Alison Kelly
Roehampton University

Contents

Chapter 1
Nobody's baby

"Take... care... of... him." The young mother's whisper was as soft as the swirling snow outside; her face as white as the sheet that covered her. Feebly she touched her newborn son, breathed a last sigh, and closed her eyes.

"She's dead!" announced Mrs. Mann, the midwife. "What a nuisance. I'll have to get Mr. Bumble."

Mr. Bumble was in charge of the workhouse – a cold, grim place for the homeless without a spark of comfort or a crumb of nourishing food. He didn't care if the inmates starved, as long as his own tummy felt warm and full three times a day.

Quickly, Mrs. Mann unclasped a gold locket from the dead woman's neck and put it around her own. Opening it, she read the name "Agnes" engraved inside.

"Another orphan brat," raged Mr. Bumble, when he saw the baby. "Who is he anyway?"

"Who knows?" Mrs. Mann yawned. "His mother walked in yesterday off the street. She must have walked some distance – her shoes were worn out. Good looking girl, too."

"He must have a name..." Mr. Bumble thought hard. "Well, I name all orphans alphabetically and the last one was Smith, so he can be Twist. Oliver Twist."

"Ooh, Mr. Bumble, you are clever," smiled Mrs. Mann, fluttering her eyelashes at him. She wrapped Oliver in a scrap of cloth, yellowed with age.

Oliver opened his mouth and roared with all the force of his baby lungs. If he'd understood he was an orphan, loved by no one, he would have cried even louder.

Chapter 2

More means less

By the time Oliver was seven he was sleeping in a dormitory with fifty other starving boys.

"I'm so hungry I could eat the boy in the next bed!" complained a tall, strong boy with wild, angry eyes.

The boy in the next bed gulped. "We must have more food," he agreed, hastily. "Let's draw straws to decide who's going to ask Mr. Bumble."

Oliver's heart was thumping as he reached out to draw his straw. He pulled it close. "Oh no!" he cried. "It's me."

Supper, as usual, was gruel – a kind of thin watery porridge with a few lumps of gristle floating in it. The boys lined up in front of Mr. Bumble who stood at one end of the dining room, a huge apron tied around his fat belly, ladling a small spoonful into each boy's bowl.

They returned to their tables to eat their food, packed on benches as tight as sardines, though not so plump. Their bowls never needed washing.

They were licked clean in seconds until they shone like polished china.

The boys sitting near Oliver kicked him under the table.

"Go on, Oliver."

"Ask NOW."

Shivering with fear, Oliver walked the length of the room. He clutched his bowl so tightly his knuckles gleamed white.

A terrible silence descended, pierced
by Oliver's slow echoing footsteps on
the stone floor. He passed table after table
of boys, their spoons laid down, their
empty bowls in front of them. Each
round-eyed boy stared at him expectantly
as he went by. Oliver guessed what they
were thinking – *I'm glad it's him, not me.*
At last he reached Mr. Bumble, who
looked down his nose at Oliver, as
though he were an insect he
wanted to squash.

Oliver forced himself
to speak. "Please sir,
I want some more,"
he whispered.

"WHAT?" shouted
Mr. Bumble.

"Please sir, I want
some more."

Mr. Bumble swelled like an evil giant. His eyes bulged with fury and his face went purple. "More? How DARE you! Wicked boy!"

He seized Oliver, hit him with the gruel ladle and threw him into the coal cellar, locking the door. "Your punishment starts here," he bellowed.

Oliver heard him stump up the steps, muttering as he went. "No one's *ever* asked for more before. Mark my words, he'll be a criminal when he grows up. That boy will hang!"

In the dark, sooty cellar, cobwebs stroked Oliver's face like creepy fingers, and rats scratched the walls. He crouched in a corner, pressing himself close to the wall. Its hard, cold surface felt almost protective in the lonely gloom. He stayed awake all night, dreading what would happen to him next.

Chapter 3

Running away

As Oliver crouched in the cellar, Mr. Bumble was nailing an advertisement to the workhouse door.

The next day, Mr. Bumble dragged
Oliver from the cellar. "There are two
men coming to see you," he said, "so
make sure you behave."

Oliver watched as the first man pulled
up outside the door, in a donkey cart
laden with soot.

"Whoah!" he shouted, hitting the
donkey on the head with a great
thump from his whip.

"Mr. Gamfield," said Mr. Bumble,
stepping out to
greet him.

BOY FOR
SALE £5

Mr. Gamfield stared at Oliver. "He's a very *small* boy. But I need an apprentice to climb chimneys and sweep out soot. Some of the chimneys are narrow and twisting. This brat will fit nicely."

"Please don't make me go," cried Oliver. "I won't go with him! I won't!"

"Don't be so insolent," said Mr. Bumble.

"I've heard about chimney sweeps," Oliver said. "You can die up a chimney. They light a fire to make you hurry down, and you get smothered in the smoke."

"Nonsense!" said Mr. Gamfield. "I just gets a nice crackling blaze going and the boys come down quicker than anything."

"Then I'll frizzle in flames. I'm not going," replied Oliver firmly.

Mr. Gamfield clambered back into his donkey cart. "I don't want a rebellious boy. You've spoiled him, Mr. Bumble."

With that, he whipped the donkey until it trotted away.

Mr. Bumble shook Oliver until his teeth rattled. "Keep your mouth shut or no one will want you," he bellowed. "You've ruined that chance. Don't ruin the next. Look! Here it comes now."

He pointed to a thin, spidery man coming up to the door.

The man had a gloomy air. "I am Mr. Sowerberry," he introduced himself. "I arrange funerals and I need help." He looked at Oliver closely. "This boy will do, but he's so thin, he's not worth five pounds. I'll give you three pounds for him. Take it or leave it."

Mr. Bumble was disgusted, but there was nothing he could do. He was eager to see the last of Oliver. "Glad you're going, Oliver. Behave, or else..." he threatened.

Back at his shop, Mr. Sowerberry showed Oliver a dusty basement. A dim light filtered in, through a grimy pane of glass barred with rusty iron rails.

"You'll sleep here, you little bag of bones," he said.

Oliver looked around the shadowy room. It was stacked with empty coffins and planks of wood. Drapes of black cloth hung from hooks in the walls, billowing occasionally in the breeze, as though first they breathed... and then were lifeless. The only place to sleep – a recess behind the coffins where a thin mattress was thrust – looked like a grave.

"And this is Noah, my apprentice," Mr. Sowerberry went on, taking him to the kitchen. "Noah, give Oliver his supper."

Noah looked cross. "What work is he going to do?" he asked, sulkily.

"He'll be a mute. He's a good-looking boy. Dressed in a top hat and mourning clothes, he'll be a credit to the business."

"Please sir, what's a mute?" asked Oliver.

"A mute walks next to the coffin at funerals and follows it to the grave. Children's funerals only. Winter's coming on – the sickly season. Always lots of children's funerals this time of year..."

Noah grinned unpleasantly when Mr. Sowerberry left them alone. "Here's your food." He handed Oliver the dog's bowl. Stuck to the side were some stinking scraps of cold fat the dog had rejected.

Oliver was so hungry, he wolfed them down.

"Pig!" mocked Noah. "Workhouse Boy! If your mother hadn't died, she'd be in prison. She must have been bad. Only bad 'uns give birth in the workhouse."

"Don't you dare say anything against my mother!" shouted Oliver.

"So? What are you going to do about it?" Noah jeered.

"This!" Oliver punched Noah hard in his flabby stomach. Noah collapsed like a crumpled balloon.

"Ow!" he squealed. "HELP! MURDER! Mr. Sowerberry? You've lost your mind, Oliver Twist. You just wait, Workhouse Boy. You'll be punished for this."

"Do what you want," replied Oliver. "I'm not staying here any longer." He raced out of the door and tore down the road, his heart pounding. "Don't let them come after me," he prayed.

Chapter 4

New friends

Oliver ran and ran until he came to a signpost. "I'll walk to London," he decided. "Perhaps I can make a better life for myself there."

He walked ten miles a day. At night he hid in hay barns and woke each morning aching and weak with hunger. The nights were worst, because there was nothing around him but darkness and loneliness.

At last he reached
the city. His sore feet were
bleeding and his clothes were
worn to shreds. He watched people
jostling around market stalls and shops,
so busy that no one noticed him.

He collapsed on a cold doorstep, too exhausted to beg. Delicious smells floated by from a bakery. Oliver staggered up to the window, where shelves groaned with piles of freshly-made bread, cakes, buns and pies. He stared at them longingly.

A boy about the same age, with sharp eyes and a swaggering walk, strolled over. "Hungry?" he asked.

"Very," gasped Oliver.

To Oliver's astonishment, the boy
pulled a wad of money out of his pocket.

"I'll get you something. Wait here."

The boy returned with a bag crammed
with hot meat pies.

"I'm Dodger," said the boy, as Oliver
gobbled the food. "You?"

"Oliver Twist."

"Got a bed tonight, Oliver?"

"No."

"Got any family?"

"No one at all."

"I know a kind gentleman who'll take you in. He won't want any rent, either."

"That's generous!" exclaimed Oliver. He followed Dodger down a maze of narrow alleys, where foul smells filled the air and swarms of ragged urchins played in slimy, oozing gutters. Men and women staggered around, cursing loudly.

It looked so dirty, Oliver almost wished
he hadn't come, but he had nowhere else
to go. Finally, they reached a crumbling
house. Dodger led him up a rickety
staircase to a dark room.

Through a cloud of sizzling fumes,
Oliver spied a gnarled old man. He was
wearing a grubby blue coat and frying
sausages over the fire.

Behind him, a group of boys danced and dodged, playing a game. The old man's coat had lots of pockets, stuffed with hankies, wallets and pens and the boys were trying to pull them out without him noticing.

"Hey, Fagin," yelled Dodger. "This is Oliver."

"Hello, Oliver." Fagin bared his teeth in a leering grin. "Want to play?"

"Yes sir," said Oliver politely. He waited until Fagin bent over the frying pan, crept up… and delicately drew out a hanky.

"You're a natural!" chuckled Fagin. "Come near the fire. Have a sausage!"

Another man stepped in, smearing the back of his dirty hand across his mouth. With him were a girl and a snarling dog with a scratched, torn face.

"Ah, Bill Sikes," drawled Fagin. "Delighted to see you! What can I do for you and Nancy?"

"Give Bullseye supper," Bill growled, kicking his dog. "And get me a drink."

"Get to work, boys," Fagin ordered. One found a bone for the dog, while Dodger gave Nancy a half-full jug of gin. She emptied it into a brimming mug and passed it to Bill.

"Bill's scary," Oliver thought, snuggling under his blanket that night. "But I'm lucky to have found new friends."

The next morning, waking in the pale half-light of dawn, Oliver saw Fagin open a chest and run his hands over necklaces, sparkling rings and shining gold coins.

Fagin turned to face Oliver's gaze. He thrust the chest back under the floor, seized a knife and pressed the blade into Oliver's neck.

"What did you see?" he hissed.

"Nothing," stammered Oliver, terrified.

"Good boy," said Fagin, letting go. "Keep quiet, or you'll be sorry. That's all I have to keep me in my old age. Do what you're told, Oliver, if you want to be happy here."

A few days later, Fagin told Oliver to go out with Dodger. They stopped by a bookshop which had a stall outside in the street. A richly-dressed gentleman had picked up a book from the stall and was reading it as hard as if he was in his study.

"See him?" asked Dodger. "Prime target. Stick by me."

With one slick move, Dodger pulled a wallet from the gentleman's coat pocket.

In that moment, Oliver saw what his new friends were. Thieves!

Chapter 5

Betrayed

The gentleman spun around, realizing he'd been robbed. "STOP THIEF!" he yelled at Oliver.

Oliver looked for Dodger but he'd vanished. Panicking, Oliver raced off, followed by every man and woman in the street.

"STOP THIEF!" they shouted,
chasing him helter-skelter through mud
and puddles, throwing sticks and stones
at his scrawny back.

Oliver, breathless, kept running until
a stone struck his head. He fell down,
stunned. "Please sir," he whispered, as the
gentleman reached him. "I'm not a thief."

The gentleman stared at him. "Hmm... Well, you look honest. Indeed, you look like–" He stopped, puzzled. "I'm sure I know that face," he murmured

"Get the police," said a passer-by.

"No. He deserves a chance," replied the gentleman. "Who are you, boy? My name's Brownlow. Perhaps I can help you. Come with me."

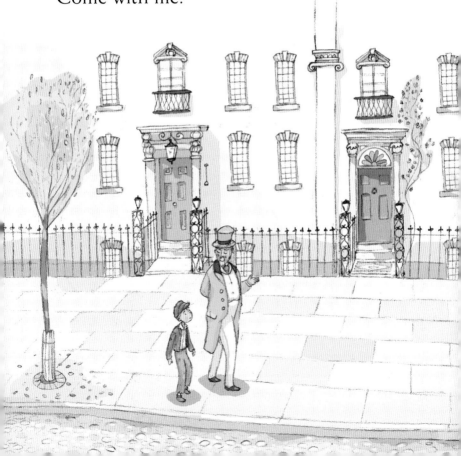

Mr. Brownlow took Oliver to his grand house. In the hallway was a portrait of a beautiful girl. Oliver stopped and stared at it, drinking it in.

"That was my niece, Agnes," said Mr. Brownlow. "She had a sad life. I wish she'd come to me for help. She must be dead now, poor girl." He looked at the portrait, then at Oliver. "I can't believe it," he muttered. "The likeness is extraordinary... Where were you born?" he asked urgently.

"In Mr. Bumble's workhouse," Oliver replied, surprised at the sudden question.

"Yes, I've heard of it," said Mr. Brownlow, nodding and looking grim. "Now, tell me about yourself."

Oliver recounted his life story, up until the moment he ran from the bookshop.

"I believe you," said Mr. Brownlow. He put his hands on Oliver's shoulders and looked down at him. "Would you like to live here and go to school?"

"Really?" gasped Oliver. "Truly?"

Mr. Brownlow laughed. "I'll have Mrs. Bedwin, my housekeeper, show you to your room."

"You poor child," sighed Mrs. Bedwin, as she took Oliver upstairs. "So dirty and ragged. Have a hot bath and I'll get you some clean clothes."

Lying in bed that night Oliver had never felt happier. And, as the weeks passed, he grew happier still. Mrs. Bedwin looked after him, from a good breakfast each morning to a hug last thing at night.

Mr. Brownlow played games with him, shared his books and taught him chess and music.

"I feel as if I'm living in a dream," thought Oliver.

A few weeks later, Mr. Brownlow summoned him to his study. "Here's five pounds and some books. Will you take them to the bookshop where we met?"

"Of course," replied Oliver. "I'll do anything for you!"

"And come straight home," Mr. Brownlow said.

"I'll run there and back again," Oliver promised. He ran down the front steps and waved goodbye to Mrs. Bedwin, who was watching him from the window.

"Bless him," she thought. "I can't bear to let him out of my sight."

Oliver whistled as he strolled down the street. Suddenly, a pair of arms seized him tightly around the neck.

"OW!" he yelled. "Let go."

"Oh, Oliver, you naughty boy! I've found you."

Oliver was astonished. It was Nancy, Bill Sikes' friend. "Nancy – is that you? What are you doing here?"

A crowd gathered, staring at them.

"He's my little runaway brother," Nancy announced in a silky, false voice.

"But…" Oliver began.

Bill Sikes shot out of a beer shop with his snarling dog and grabbed Oliver.

"Watch him, Bullseye," he hissed. Bullseye seized Oliver's leg and hung on to it with his sharp teeth.

"I don't belong to these people!" shouted Oliver, struggling to get away. "I have to go back to Mr. Brownlow."

But Nancy quickly covered his mouth until he nearly suffocated.

Bill dragged him through the alleyways, Bullseye growling at Oliver's every step, until they reached Fagin's attic.

"Good of you to drop in, Oliver," drawled Fagin sarcastically.

"Fancy clothes," laughed Dodger.

"Expensive books! We'll sell everything," crowed Fagin. He examined Oliver's pockets. "Aha! Even better. Here's five pounds."

"Mine," growled Bill.

"No, mine, surely," contradicted Fagin, but Bill snatched it away.

"It's Mr. Brownlow's," said Oliver bitterly. "Let me go," he begged. "Or Mr. Brownlow will think I'm a thief."

Fagin patted his head. "We'll make you one soon."

"NO!" Oliver shouted. "Why do you want me anyway?"

"So you can't tell tales," sneered Bill. "Once you're one of us, you won't dare tell the police. Now shut up."

Chapter 6

A robbery

Oliver was forced to wear filthy rags again. For several days the thieves made him stay in the attic, watched over by the vicious Bullseye.

Every time Oliver went near the door, Bullseye snarled, showing his sharp fangs.

"Don't set the dog on him, Bill," Nancy begged. "You've got Oliver back. You don't have to frighten him now."

"Oh don't I?" snarled Bill. He brandished a pistol. "See this, Oliver?"

Oliver nodded nervously.

"It's loaded. If you don't do what you're told, I'll fire. Understand?"

"Yes, Bill," said Oliver, trembling.

"Good. There's a job I want to do tonight. Big house, loaded with silver and jewels. They keep a small window open and I need a scrap of a boy to slip through it and undo the door locks."

"He means what he says about the gun," advised Fagin. "Don't try and cross Bill Sikes."

When night fell, Bill dragged Oliver to the house. They hid under a bush until the church clock struck midnight. It was intensely dark.

Bill hoisted Oliver up to a tiny window. "Get in," he hissed.

"Please don't make me steal," implored Oliver.

Sikes raised his fist. "Do it, or I'll bash your head in."

He shoved Oliver through the window, lit a lantern and handed it to him. "Open the front door," he ordered. "There's a bolt at the top you won't reach, so stand on one of the chairs. Remember, you're in my gunshot range."

Oliver saw Bill's pistol aimed at
him. He had no choice: he crept
inside and went to unlock the door.

As he slid back the bolt, he
heard Bill running around to
the front of the house.

"I must warn the family,
somehow," Oliver thought.
"I don't care what
happens to me."
And he dropped
the lantern with
a clatter.

After that, everything seemed to
happen at once. Bill burst in to grab
Oliver, a man appeared with a gun,
and both men fired.

Oliver screamed, caught in the
crossfire. He clutched his arm and
saw his sleeve turn red.

Bill dragged him
outside. "You fool," he
growled. "They'll be after us. RUN!"

But Oliver, his arm throbbing, lagged behind. Bill flung him into a ditch. "You're too slow," he yelled down at him. "You can die here."

When Bill finally reached Fagin's house, Nancy rushed up to him. "How did it go?" she asked.

"Disaster," said Bill curtly. "Get me a drink."

"Where's the boy, Bill?"

"Dying in a ditch somewhere."

"You can't leave him there," Nancy
cried. "I'll go and find him."

Bill lurched to his feet. "Don't you dare,
Nancy!" But Nancy had already grabbed
her cloak and was running through the
door. A crafty look spread over Bill's face.

"After her, Bullseye," he ordered. "She
won't get away with this."

Nancy ran to the house Bill had tried to rob and searched everywhere for Oliver. At last she found him, weak and shivering.

"Thank you for coming," he muttered. She quickly bandaged his bleeding arm with her shawl. "I found your friend Mr. Brownlow. I'll take you to him," she whispered. "He'll be waiting for us on London Bridge."

"I don't believe you," Oliver said.
"It's a trick."

"It isn't, Oliver, I promise. I met Mr.
Brownlow yesterday. It's all arranged."

"Why are you doing this?"

"I've worked for Fagin since I was
little. I don't want you to suffer like me."

"Stay with me," Oliver urged her.
"Mr. Brownlow will look after you too.
We could both start a new life."

"I can't leave Bill," Nancy shrugged.
"I know he's bad, but I love him.
Besides," she added, "I've
been a thief all my life. It's
too late to change now."

"It's never too late,"
said Oliver.

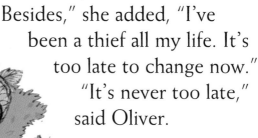

They hurried through the dark streets where flickering gas lamps shone eerie shafts of light on the cobbles.

Neither of them saw the dog following them – a dog with a scratched torn face and an eager snarling mouth. And behind the dog, a man, who moved with silent, stealthy footsteps through the shadows.

Chapter 7

The secret of the locket

They reached the bridge at dawn. Mr. Brownlow was waiting, just as Nancy had promised. "Run!" she cried to Oliver.

Oliver dashed forward. He'd almost reached Mr. Brownlow's outstretched arms when Nancy's frightened voice made him turn around.

"W-why did you follow me, Bill?" Nancy stuttered. "I told no tales – I'd never grass on you."

"You took the boy away," Bill bellowed. "You betrayed me, Nancy. I can't ever trust you again."

Then Oliver heard Nancy scream. "No! Please, Bill, NO!"

BANG! A pistol shot exploded and
Nancy slumped lifeless to the ground. Bill
swore and closed his eyes. "I had to kill
her," he muttered.

Oliver was frozen to the spot with terror.

"I'm here, Oliver," said Mr. Brownlow,
reassuringly. "Come to me. Don't look."

By now, a crowd had appeared, drawn
by the sound of the pistol shot. Bill fled
from the bridge, desperate to escape.

The crowd tore
after him. In a panic,
Bill climbed the drainpipe
of a nearby house and
scaled the roof.

He grabbed a rope that was dangling
from its chimney, intending to swing
over to the roof of the house opposite.
Quickly, he made a loop and slipped it
over his head. But before he could bring
it down his body and under his arms,
a policeman sounded his whistle below.

"Stop him!" cried a woman.
"He's getting away."

Bill lost his balance and
tumbled off the roof, the
rope tightening around
his neck. In seconds,
he was dead, his
body swaying
in mid-air.

Bullseye ran back and forth, howling dismally. Then the dog leaped at the dead man, trying to reach him. Instead, he dashed his head on a stone windowsill and fell to the ground. The dog was as dead as his master.

Mr. Brownlow held Oliver firmly in his arms. Oliver couldn't stop shaking.

"Nothing can hurt you now," Mr. Brownlow told him. "You're safe. Bill deserved that, for what he did to Nancy."

"Poor Nancy," Oliver sobbed.

"Yes, she was a brave girl." He hugged Oliver tightly. "Listen, Oliver, I have good news for both of us. I went to see Mr. Bumble and he gave me this." He handed Oliver a gold locket. "Open it."

Oliver looked at the inscription inside. "Agnes," he read.

"Mrs. Mann, the midwife who was with your mother at the workhouse, stole this locket from her. Later, Mrs. Mann married Mr. Bumble. That's how he discovered the locket."

"Was Agnes my mother?" Oliver asked.

"Yes. Your mother and my niece. I gave her the locket many years ago – I recognized it at once. You remember her portrait at home? You look just like her."

Mr. Brownlow hugged Oliver again. "You're my boy now," he said.

"Do I really belong to you?" Oliver asked, hardly daring to believe it.

Mr. Brownlow smiled. "You really do. Please God, your unhappy life is over forever. Let's go, Oliver. Mrs. Bedwin is longing to see you again."

And, hand-in-hand, they walked home.

Charles Dickens 1812-1870

Charles Dickens lived in London, England, during the reign of Queen Victoria. When he was 12, he was sent to work in a factory for a few months. Dickens hated it and never forgot how miserable life was for the poor.

Oliver Twist, like Dickens' other novels, was published in several parts, and Dickens wrote in lots of cliff-hangers, to keep his readers hooked.

Usborne Quicklinks

To find out more about Dickens and life in Victorian times, go to the Usborne Quicklinks website at **www.usborne.com/quicklinks** and enter the title of this book. Please follow the internet safety guidelines at the Usborne Quicklinks website.

Designed by Natacha Goransky
Additional design by Hayley Wells
Series editor: Lesley Sims
Series designer: Russell Punter